HER DIARY OF METANOIA

EKAM'S SPIRITUAL CONVERSATIONS

BY

EKAMJOT KAUR

ISBN 978-93-5438-955-9

Published in India 2020 by Pencil

A brand of

One Point Six Technologies Pvt. Ltd.

123, Building J2, Shram Seva Premises,

Wadala Truck Terminal, Wadala (E)

Mumbai 400037, Maharashtra, INDIA

E connect@thepencilapp.com

W www.thepencilapp.com

Author biography

Hello all Amazing Readers.

I am Ekamjot Kaur (Ekam). An 18 year old teenage girl, who is just trying to pen her words in the form of poetry.

"HER DIARY OF METANOIA" is my debut book. Hope you all will like this, some of you may feel relatable, and yeah I'll be so glad to gwt your feedbacks at my mail address dhillon25ek@gmail.com

-HAPPY READING

Contents

Acknowledgements 07

Kuch toa lok kahenge 08

Mazaak hai kya..10

Apparently, this world is not a wish
granting factory 13

Sunsets are Witness..15

It was not easy 16

I Never told you 18

You were trouble 20

Lets keep on the count..22

Make a promise 25

Yes you are, I know 27

You are an Idiot 29

One word, Not enough 31

Be Loved, Beloved...33

I see you standin.... watchin.... over me 35

I never expressed, but...37

Leave na, let it be a secret....................................39

Now, I do not love 41

I am leaving soon 43

Is that day, Today..45

One Last Day 47

I Love It When 50

Would not be able to love 52

But, You left without a goodbye 54

Yes, I am scared 56

Plan of Destiny..58

More of you, Less of me 61

Not too old 63

See, You are smiling - a song fiction....................65

They have never left- A song fiction.....................68

143 Pages Apart- A song fiction 71

Acknowledgements

This book contains 30 poems on different themes and topics. Some will make you feel a sudden twitch, some of them will take you back into the world of your memories, while some of you will find them so relatable that you'll start grinning like an idiot after reading them and some words will tell you to

"Drouse the old,and Embrace the new"

My journey till this was inside my comfort zone, with my family who made me strong enough, loved me constantly, supported me everytime and for that I would like to thank my parents Mrs.Sukhvir Kaur and Mr.Updesh Singh. Furthermore I would like to thank everyone out there who inspired me including my friends and my school especially my maternal grandfather Sardar Harpal Singh Sekhon.

I wish my Maternal Grandmother was here today to see me smiling with my debut book,

"HER DIARY OF METANOIA"

At last, a special thank to PENCIL team for providing me the platform.

This one for you VILLIAN.

Kuch toa lok kahenge.

.....Kuch toa log kahenge,

Logon ka kaam hai kehna....

Chodo bekaar ki baaton mein,

Kahin beet na jaaye rehna..........

A song clearly known to all,

But we don't implement it in real life..!

Are our minds still so small??

Why are we so scared to take initiative?

When our bodies are filled with zeal,

And our minds are so creative....!

For popularity we thrive,

Then why always choose the easiest way for our life's long drive???

Why don't we try something different, something new?

Not everyone rise up in this world,

Such courageous people are very few....!

The world is ready to judge us,

To oppose you, people are lined up in the queue....

But no one can affect your strength,

Until your own belief is with you.....!

You are standing like a pillar,

And the world is trying to push you down...

Don't loose your hope dear,

Your parents are with you and you are their head's invisible crown...!

Let the people say whatever they want,

Don't get sad just because of there hateful taunts....

.........Arre..........

Kuch toa log kahenge,

Nhi toa wo zinda kaise rahenge...

Mazaak hai kya

We are living organisms too,

why the word "RAPE" brings our life to an end?

Arre mazaak hai kya?

Or is this the world's new trend??

What the hell is people's problem?

"You are a girl"

Oh my goodness,they start judging your dresscode,

even before you enter this world.

That NIRBHAYA girl,

What was her fault?

She had dreams too,

To live a happy life, Not such kind of assault.

Recently highlighted one

Priyanka Reddy's Rape,

Oh comm'on you can't accuse the dress code,

Not this time,for god's sake.

A small baby girl in diappers,

Or a married woman in full wear,

Whatever the dresscode, whatever the age,

I know it's disgusting but these rapists do not care!

Delhi, the capital of our country,

Or you can call it the rape capital too,

Everyday the rape cases are increasing,

Most of them are hidden,

and those we get to know are very few.

What do we usually do?

when we get to know about any such case,

We just show some sympathy,

and put a temperory grief on our face.

Arre! Mazaak Hai Kya?

After 4 years of rape, rapist ko milti hai szza,

Ye insaaf bhi koi insaaf hai kya??

When a girl is raped,

Her dress, her behavior, her character is accused,

The whole fault is her's; She is the one...

And the rapists????

Na..Na..Na.. don't say anything to them,

they are society's precious diamonds.

A girl got raped,

In hindi this act is most GHINAUNA....!

Nhi, what these rapists think about a girl?

Is she just a "CHAABI WALA KHILAUNA" ??

Rape problem is increasing everyday in the country, koi new riwaaz hai kya?

Girls ko Whore or Slut mein identify kr k uski life ko hell bnaane walo,

"ARRE! KOI MZAAK HAI KYA?"

Apparently, this world is not a wish granting factory.

Leaving you is not easy; not at all,

Waving you goodbye is not my cup of tea,

I wanted you by my side everytime i fall,

But smile na; soon m gonna set you free.

For once; i'll break you down,

I'll make you feel low,

Don't worry! This time you'll get someone
you deserve,

I know.

Everytime i look at you,

I smile with my eyes wet,

My brain start playing the tape recorder,

Since the day we met.

The day i'll leave

The sky will cry,

The winds filled with sorrow

Will make you feel dry,

The shed down dandileons will swirl the
same direction,

I know u'll look at the sky,
And from there i'll record your reaction.

I wished to become your only and forever,
Apparently neither this world is a wish
granting factory,
Nor it can be; EVER.!.

Sunsets are Witness

"Zindagi ek safar hai suhana...
Yahan kal kya ho kisne jana?"

The very famous song known to all,
The point is very deep,
But let me explain u guys in small....!

A cheerful smile can also have a sorrow heart,
No one knows here what future holds apart?
Everyone have a problem in there life,
But some cowards try to end them with rope and
some do so using knife.......!

What we are and what we do,
Our innerself clearly know,
Obviously we gonna get the fruit,
According to the seeds we sow.....!

Not together but always connected,
Whether happy or sad...! It will leave u affected.....
Live your life like a jouney not like any race,
U complain that no one cares about u?
Oye.....!
Sunsets are the witness of your every happy and sad
phase..

It was not easy

It have been so long,

And literally i have acted so strong,

Now this patience is not enough,

It wasn't easy to let you go with a fakesmile,

It was really; really very tough

We were each other's secret holder,

And the way you use to say "u can do it"
rises me up n makes me bolder,

But the day you told me about your new friend,

It wasn't easy for me to congrats you,

But happiness is what i was forced to pretend......!

No matter we were miles apart,

You was the one who hold my heart,

Instead of calling me your love when you
called me just friend,

It wasn't easy for me to reply you hello,

That day my charming smiles met a deadly end........!

Msg/calls notifications from you were all
enough to make my day,

Now we act like strangers; really don't know
what to say,

I have learnt to hide my tears behind this happy face,

It wasn't easy for me to say you goodbye,

But still i crave for your love in my life's daily
race.......!

Hey, don't worry i won't ever blame you,

"Forever is just a word" in this line there is
nothing new,

But i guess we decided to be an exception;
And to prove it wrong,

It wasn't easy for me to face the world again,

But my daily tears and loosing fears r the one
who made me strong....

I Never told you.

The days we spend smiling together,

Those days were my favourite when,

I was your happy weather,

I never told you because i was scared,

You were the only one for whom i cared.

The days you were upset,

I tried to make you laugh,

And most of the time they were successful;
I bet,

You were my heart's 2nd half,

I never told you that you were the reason
of my smiles,

As i desired to walk with you hand-in-hand
for infinite miles.

We use to roast one another,

Each and every day,

You were in my every text; in my every call,

And we were forever friends; u say,

I never told you but for me,

You was more than just friend,

As I knew; that will take our relation to a dead end..

You know what?

You were my favourite song,

You were the one at whom I can stare
without blinking,

Life long!

You were the one who makes me happy;
who makes me strong,

I never told you that i love you so much,

Just to prevent our friendship getting wrong.

I know its not easy,

But for "us" i will pretend,

And i will pretend till the end

You were trouble

One winter morning
Sitting beside the fireplace,
Remembring the old times
And the first come was your face.

Once upon a time
A few mistakes ago,
That chapter of my life with you
Where i never want to go.

It was the day when i saw you
A flashback started like of a pegion and a dove,
And it was my blunder
When i disguised infatuation as true love.

That time was so good
When you kept saying
'You are mine, You are mine",
But now its clear that you were just pretending
Well now its fine.

It was my mistake
When i ignored every sign,

Which were the warning ne to stop

And telling me 'No, you are not mine".

Then the time flies

And i started noticing the change,

I realised all efforts were from my side

Everytime i texted, you only replied,

Isn't it strange?

I wasted my time to get you,

And realised that i was a loser even after my win,

I can't blame you

As I already knew,

You were a trouble when you walked in.

Lets keep on the count

New days and new drama,

Ohh lemme wear my new dress,

I'm still in old pyjaamas,

Omg! It's already 8,

He's on the way

I won't be late.

I'll wear his fav red,

'Its the color of love' once he said,

I m prepared that how to dance,

He's on the way

This time i won't miss the chance.

Red lips and rosy cheeks

Completely ready I am,

Just look!

There comes my handsome man,

Properly uniformed in suit and tie,

Finally he's here

God! Help me 'not to die'.

Ohh my drop-dead gorgeous lady,

These were the words he said,

I can't get through these

They are still running in my head,

Ready to go for my date,

He's with me now

My lovely handsome mate.

My insecurities rise up

When a young lady met him and said WHATSUPP,

He told me "she's my old good friend"

Well, what the hell is this new trend?

Holy shit i saw her again,

This time on this FB page,

Usually i'm a calm girl but now

I'm burning hot in RAGE,

OMG! who is she?

I get drunk on jealousy.

Here begin the last part,

When he decided to break apart,

He thought i'll cry in pain,

O Man! U don't know m already insane,

Don't come back once you go,

Well, who's my new date?

Do you know?

One more handsome man

Here i found,

He's now my lover number....?

Well let's keep on the count

Make a promise

People say I look upset,
People say I am mad
But wait! It was a promise
That I'll always keep you happy
And you'll never let me remain sad.

My heart is not feeling good,
It is because of this aloof time?
But wait! It was a promise
That I'll always love you the same and
You'll always be mine.

I wake up and cleared my throat,
But still my voice is not in tone.
Oh wait! It was a promise
That I'll only sing for you; under the moonlight,
When the nature will be at peace and we both
will be alone.

I am out of words,
I am not able to make any good line.
But wait! I have to write
It was a promise I did to myself,

That I'll always write for you something new
everytime.

In today's world everyone is saying
"Chle jaate hain rishte puraane kisi naye
ke aa jaane se"
But wait! Let me make one more promise now
I'll show you that I came in your life not to leave
but to stay.

I can't swear fake,
And you know this from very start.
And today I want you to make a promise,
That no matter what but you'll never unlove me;
And will never set me apart.

If you agree on this,
Then it'll be my biggest win
So, what's your choice?
Hey say na; are you in??

Yes you are, I know

I met you so many times before,

But this time it is not like so,

You have become the person; i adore!

You are my first love,

Yes; you are; i know

May be, i speak too much,

May be, my every compliment have a filmy touch,

But now for me; its like I am a penguine and
you are my snow,

And wooosh! I have fallen for you,

Yes i have; i have; i know...

Isn't it like a day dream?

That i have started loving someone more than my
icecream,

Now every love song i listen to is relatable though,

And you are becoming so irresstible,

Yes you are; you are ; i know..!

You may not like my this behavior at all,

But i really don't need any answer for my
proposal call!

I am scared of expectations that may grow,

And i may never ask you about this,

Never ever; I know...

As per the rule all this will end with passage of time,

You will find your match ; and i'll loose the right to call you "mine",

Can't say; to wave you goodbye i'll be strong enough or filled with sorrow,

Yes, i can't;

And this is what i don't know

You are an Idiot

I have a secret to tell,

All of me; loves all of you

I know now you'll yell and say,

You tell me this everyday; there's nothing new.

Today i want to thank you,

For?

For being mine

For supporting me everytime

For telling me 'Don't worry, everything will be fine'

Thankyou for making me believe

that not everyone is here to leave.

So in my messy life,

Who are you?

A great gift?

A magical bless?

Yes! A big big big yess!

Paint me yellow

And call me sunshine,

Whether far away from you

But i'll be always yours and you'll be mine.

How much i miss you only i know,
Your every single act makes me love you more
and more.
Your smiley emojis
Makes me blush,
Your sudden 'oye '
Makes my butterflies rush.

Only if i could have a ginnie
I could wish you were here,
Or i was with you there,
Or we were together anywhere.

I have a complaint from you
Let me tell you to clear your sophistication,
You are an idiot,
And you love an idiot,
So that makes you more idiot, just by association.

At every pierced piece of my soul,
You and your love acts like a cure.
I belong to no one but
Yes,
I would never, never mind
Being yours.

One word, Not enough.

It's not possible to give one single statement
about love,

Not at all.

Coz, for some its as huge as a 'confusing maze'

For others its like a small and mere so called 'craze'.

Love is like a 'worship'

When your 'devotion' is strong.

SRK said love is 'dosti',

Correct me if I am wrong.

That 'tenderness' and 'fondness' regarding
one person,

For some its 'adulate' for others it is a 'passion'.

I met someone about 20 years back,

It felt so 'beautiful' that my whole hatred got
packed into a 'sac'.

It was so 'celestial' that

'Goodbyes' and 'heartbreaks' were not defined.

But as soon it left,

I lost myself

Where is that 'enderment' now?

I 'hope' i could find.

They say the love that leave is 'fake',

An 'inclinated' 'illusion' is all what it make.

But sometimes loving someone is letting them go,

Love is not 'bitter', but its aftermath causes 'pain',

This is all that we know.

Sometimes love is disguised as infatuation,

That is where 'betrayal' commence,

Then it 'hurt' a person so much,

And boom!! end of the love 'suspense'.

Love is when you make someone your 'priority',

And everytime what first comes to your mind is
'loyality'.

Sometimes your true love

Makes you 'nervous'

Makes you 'happy'

Makes you 'cry'

Makes you 'blush'

Makes you 'speechless'

Love is not about breakups or patchups,

Love is not 'complicated' or 'mess'

It is just a 'feeling' that is 'eternal'

And yes it is a 'bless'.

Be Loved, Beloved

I talk to the moon,

it knows every secret of mine.

But my love is still a mystery to it,

And I guess it's fine.

I thought so much,

What should I write?

What should I write?

Then I just closed my eyes,

And let my heart decide.

Thinking about you is a

kind of meditation to my heart,

I want to tell you that how much do I Love You,

But Ohh God, from where do I start?

Let me commence with your alluring smile,

O god it is so irresistable,

No matter how much i try.

I tell everyone out there,

"I am OK"

"Tell me what's it?" You say because

you can easily detect my lie.

I know this world is not a wish granting factory,

But I got you as the best gift ever.

I don't know what the future hold?

But one thing is clear,

I'll never regret loving you, NEVER EVER.

Love that we cannot have

is the one that

Lasts the longest,

Hurts the deepest,

Yet, Feels the strongest,

I know I am gonna meet you one day,

Till that 'Be Loved, Beloved'

Is all that I wanna say.

I see you standin.... watchin.... over me

"I see u standin',

Watchin' over me"

There is something

i wanna tell you since so long,

Now the condition is such,

That my heart itself is singing a song.

Whenever you are not in front of my eyes,

To find you; my heart do unlimited tries,

Whether physically present or not,

I know you will always be my side,

And this is my biggest pride !

I know you are there,

You are with me everytime....!

My heart beats faster and cheeks blush,

Whenever you call me "MINE"......!

You are the one that calms my soul,

In my life's everyday race,

Whenever i am sad; u console,

You are my happy face!

When you smile,

My heart rejoice,

Whenever i look at you; I realise,

I have the world's best choice

I know soon we gonna get so far from each other,

But my love for you will be same forever,

This love is the purest for whole life,

But i won't ask u to feel the same for me,

Never ever......!

Neither I will forget you,

Nor my heart will be,

Once again I be yours when

"I'll see you standin',

Watchin' over me"

I never expressed, but

I still wait for your "hey",

When we started; i still remember that day,

We stood together in every right; in every wrong,

I never expressed;but for you my heart was always

singing a song...

I remember the day we laughed alot,

I remember the time you told me that i am your

happy spot,

But it was only the matter of time,

I never expressed; but i always wanted you to be

forever mine.....

You were the one who could understand my mood,

You were the one with whom i loved sharing my

food,

Whenever you became sad,

I was off too,

I never expressed; but i always prayed for a happy

you....!

I wish one day we could start again,

Once again wanna listen to you;shouting my

wierdo name,

You never get it thay i always wanted to be with you,
I will never express it; but i am still and will forever
love you

Leave na, let it be a secret.

Look you are blushing,

Mom asked me in a teasy way,

How could i tell her that its because of you,

How could I say?

Can I read aloud your name?

Leave na; let it be a secret for one more day!

My behavior is changing,

I keep smiling all day long,

The upset me search for your happy text,

And yeah! Here back i am strong,

Can i disclose it to everyone?

Leave na; Let it be a secret; it is more fun..

I really can't ignore you,

Its more like I am Mr. Bean and you are
my teddy bear,

My heart is singing a song for you,

Oye Mr. Teddy, Can you hear?

Can i shout about the relation we share?

Leave na; let it be a secret,

Anyone else knows or not; i know you are
completely aware..

Our morning starting with sweet text,

Our night ending with childish fight,

Only you own the license of teasing me,

No one else have this right...

Can i share all this with my bestfriend?

Leave na; let it be a secret,

I never want all this to end..!

You cracked a lame joke,

Still the level of my laughter is unbearable,

Whether this world will be same or not but
feelings for you will be forever stable....

Can i tell the world that i love you even
more than my chocolate?

Leave na; let it be a secret,

My love for you is something this world
won't be able to calculate....

Now, I do not love

It is different now,

I have regained the happy me; WOW!

Now i don't breakdown

When i listen to any sadsong

Now i have stop thinking

That its my fault or i m wrong

Now i don't think of you

Not at all,

I know you are not returning

Whether its winter or autumn fall.

Now your name don't give me butterflies,

Now I accepted the truth that

It was only me who made unlimited tries

Now i don't think of the tine

When thiss all start,

The bitter fact remained is that

We both are now totally apart

Now i don't look at your pics

And feel nostalgic

Now i know u are happy
May be alone or with another chick

Now i don't read our old chats
To have a smile "persisted"
One day i too will forget that
U ever existed

Now i don't love you,
Look i m giving a titter now!
But it this really that easy?
If No; why? If Yes; How?

I am leaving soon

My doremon without any gadget,

The one who's with me every time,

I really feel blessed that,

I am yours and you are mine,

I wish i could feel this forever,

I am leaving soon,

Can't stop this devil time however!

You are my addiction,

My favourite person afterall,

I can share everything with you,

Either big or small!

This all gonna end forever,

I am leaving soon,

But my vibes will not leave u alone; never ever!

I am really strong enough,

I will leave with a smile on my face,

But waving you bye is really tough,

Watching you in tears will be my life's worst phase,

For you; emotions will not be really easy to handle,

But be prepared naa!

I am leaving soon,

I wish for me every sunday you will burn a candle!

People say when your loved ones leave,

They leave a hole in your heart,

But when you'll feel such just look at the stars,

The brightest star twinkling will be me,

Indicating that we both can never be apart,

Till then can we just pretend i am not going anywhere,

I know i am leaving soon,

But i don't want you to cry,

Not even to shed a single tear!

I know its not easy,

But you have to try,

You have to promise me,

That u would not cry,

I am leaving everyone soon,

But this one is only for you my one n only moon,

I won't get too much filmy the day i'll meet you for the last time,

But "Ishhhhhh! Haaye mai marjaavaan" my cheeks won't stop blushing after facing you,

Please don't mind

Is that day, Today.

You say when you see me smiling,

Your heart bounces and rejoice

Is that day today?

When i should confess that

I am craving to hear I Love You in your voice.

Looking into your eyes

Makes me nervous but still i want to do it over
and over again,

Is that day today?

When you should tell me that yes

You too feel butterflies when

Someone takes my name.

This time i am tired

This time I am feeling alone

Is that day today?

When i should tell you that

I'm so scared of isolation and is searching
for your clone.

I want an escape from all this

I am distracting myself by listening to my
favourite song,

Is that day today?

When i should ask you to sit with me to listen
to my favourite lines

And sing along.

I am feeling sadness in my bones,

I am feeling empty without you and this is
something i can't take lightly,

Is that day today?

When i should tell you that

I want you by my side

I want you to embrace my scars and hug me tightly.

I want to go ahead in life

I want to discover everything new,

But is that day today?

When i should accept the reality

That there's no room for someone else

Because I am still holding on to you.

Somedays i felt lucky

Somedays days were happy; sad were few,

And yes today is the day

When i must confess that

It took so long to find

But you came exactly when I needed you.

One Last Day

I know the time is tough

I know i'm giving you immense pain,

I'll try my best to sort everything

Just give me one last day

I won't let your efforts go in vain.

I don't want that day to come

When you'll miss my texts

And when with teary eyes you'll look at the sky,

Just give me one last day

I'm still asking myself that what was your fault?

Why you? Why !??

Waving you a casual goodbye is not fair na?

Ok! So let me sing a love song,

Just give me one last day to complete its lyrics

Before i leave i want to sing it for you

And want you to sing along.

Okay! Okay! I know i'm a kind of idiot

I trouble you manytimes,

You figure out the truth behind my every "I am fine".

Everytime i lie - u identify

I hesitate to tell you the truth coz' it makes you cry.
Just give me one last day
I want to make everything good,
Just once; let me try.

I'm not wierd
I'm just a book of some kinda adventures
You've never read before,
But you understand my silence more that my words,
Just give me one last day
I want you to love me more.

One more day passed taking me near to the end,
Me, my pen, my diary and your thoughts,
Looking through the window
And o god! I am still lost.
I promise to write poems for you,
Just give me one last day to pen something new,
I'll read it aloud from the heaven for you.

And if you'll ever miss me
Come to my grave
To greet me "Hii",
The cold breeze will give a soft touch on your cheeks
And it will be a hint that i am nearby.
Just give me one last day to set up some sort of sign

Kind of indication that'll tell you that where
ever i am; I am fine.

Just give me one last day

I want you to once again identify my soothing lie,

Just give me one last day to tell you that 'All of me
loves All of you',

Before the day I die.

I Love It When

I love it when
You say You are mine

I love it when
You come to me to spend your time

I love it when
You send me morning text

I love it when
You compliment me the best

I love it when
You wait for me before saying goodbye

I love it when
You call me a wierdo instead of saying Hii

I love it when
You schold me for being insane

I love it when
You send emoji with my name

I love it when
You make me feel as your happy place

I love it when

You respect my privacy and gives me space

I love it when

To end our fight u say me I LOVE YOU

I love it when

You listen to my same story 100th time and everytime pretend like its new

I love it when

You make my cheeks blush

I love it when

You said

"Thats enough for today 'HUSSHH!!

' "

Would not be able to love

Remember; one day you said,

You'll not leave me ever,

You said; you are the one,

Who'll make be believe in "FOREVER",

This become a lie; all in one go,

I won't be able to love anyone else again,

And you are the reason that made me say so.

I was trying so hard,

So that i could make you stay,

But you left me into broken pieces,

I'm sorry now i've nothing to say,

It took me time to realise that all that was
an illusion,

I won't be able to love anyone again,

You made "LOVE" my life's biggest confusion..

I wish i had a time machine,

So that I could rewind the time,

Wish I could bring those moments back,

In which you were only mine,

Why u lied me that u'll never be leaving,

I won't be able to love anyone again,

In process to forget all those memories my
heart is still bleeding.

You know what my best friend warned?
"Nothing is HUMESHA",
But i a fool, challenged to prove him wrong,
Unfortunately he won, he won, O LORD!
I won't be able to love anyone again,
Another heartbreak is something my soul
can't afford.

I loved you more than myself this is what my
fault was,
I wish i had never done that,
Because all that had brought my life to a sudden
pause,
Now my life is like a maze- round n round,
I won't be able to love anyone else,
Bcoz; still you are everywhere i look but
nowhere to be found!
Nowhere to be found!

But, You left without a goodbye.

My only secret holder,

The one in my heart's every folder,

My screams;my cries,

And to make me laugh your unlimited tries!

All of sudden this stops,

My heart is still asking why?

I was trying my best to love you,

But woww; you left me without saying goodbye....!

I thought we both were very close,

You will return to me; i still hope,

I wish i could rewind the time,

But; you left me without saying goodbye,

When i was thinking that you will be forever mine...

I wish i never get high on feelings,

Your absence is a kind of disease; from which
i am dealing,

Can i call? I really miss your voice,

But; you left me without saying goodbye,

May be i wasn't a your choice.....

It is said that happy memories hurt the most,

Now my heart's sorrow show is going on and
you are its host,

Your small texts took my heart's biggest room,

But; you left me without saying goodbye,

When i was wishing for you from my moon......

I had seen 'forever' in your eyes,

I never knew that one day all those promises
will become lies,

Don't worry about me i'll be alright,

No matter that you left even without waving a bye,

Moon needs time to be full again,

So do i; to heal my pain,

My brain is compelling me to forget your name,

But still my heart wants you back; again.....

Yes, I am scared.

Whenever I get notifications; that u texted me "hey",

OMG! my eyes start shining and about my happiness; I have nothing to say,

But yes, i am scared!

I am scared that these notifications will stop coming one day...

Haha! Your non-sarcastic jokes,

On which i use to laugh!

And your teasy texts;

That makes a joyful blast,

Yes, I am scared,

I am scared that these activities will not 'long-last'...!

When you ask me 'how are you?'

And I text you 'i am fine',

The only person who know the reality behind that text is you;

And this is what makes me believe that you are still MINE,

But Yes; i am scared,

I am scared that one day,

You will end all this and will get a new valentine....

Hey; I love you,

No I love u more,

And again yes i am scared,

I am scared that one day,

I'll be the one whom you will ignore..

Is "Forever" a word?

Or is it just an illusion?

But yes i am scared,

I am scared that soon the giggles in us will change into awkward silence,

And again "love" will become my life's worst confusion

Plan of Destiny

English poem with beautiful title,

Is what you gonna read now......

Telling this in start is vital,

So that at the end you guys should say "wow"......

....It's a story of love,

a story that begin with hate...

....a story of meeting of two souls,

but ending with separation in fate.....

The girl as soft as petals of a flower,

A boy injured by his destiny's scars...

They met on an unusual day,

The first word muttered by the girl was "hey".....!

The day wasn't bloomed as shown in film,

Sky was covered with spooky clouds and

all the lights were dim.....

The boy's eyes brightened,

The girl was a little frightened...

It was unusually insane,

As both of them experienced a feeling of pain.....

Nothing was said by the boy and he walked away,

The girl examined his walk,

There was something that startled her,

Something strangely mock...!

............It was a mystery that the destiny wanted

to say............

Next it was a full moon night,

The boy didn't followed his daily routine...

He went to the dark woods,

Where no one else was ever seen...

The girl followed the boy's way,

Unaware of where he was going..

She doesn't know it was her last day,

The DEATH PLANT was about to ripe which

she herself was sowing.....

As soon she reached at the bank of lake,

She realised that it was her life's biggest mistake....

The person she use to love was not a boy,

He was a WEREWOLF,

A real one...!...not a toy...!

The werewolf was confused why

The girl wasn't running away,

the girl was standing still ,

smiling at the boy,

she was heartbroken and nothing was left to say......

The boy inside the werewolf loved the girl too,

but werewolf was heartless,

he didn't know what to do ??

He jumped over the girl and killed her without

any fear ,

Suddenly the spooky clouds covered the sky.....

and the moon disappeared........!

The boy regain himself and saw what he did.....

The day he met her soulmate was the day she

got killed....!

So this was the story,

The moon's agitate....

Btw who was responsible for this?

The boy's fate or the werewolf's hate???

More of you, Less of me.

Omg! Are you fine?

You were looking gloomy in a dream of mine.

You good?

-"Oh yes absolutely"

Then stop scaring me by coming in my every dream,

Because always it's more of you and less of me.

Hey tomorrow you are having your test,

Go and sleep now, and yes All the very Best.

-"Test is so easy I'm fully prepared".

No need to stay just go and take rest.

Well why do i prefer you even more than my
favorite icecream.

Why is it everything more of you and less of me??

Hello beta, kese ho?

And he said I am fine.

But I was so clear that something was not
OK this time.

Well I knew there was something wrong,

Coz my gut feelings were really so strong.

Tell na! Iss teddy bear k Mr. Bean,

You know you can't hide

As everytime it's more of you and less of me.

Oh please don't even try,

You really don't know how to act.

Everytime I identify your lie,

And you know it's the fact.

Still you call me an Idiot,

Well this is so mean.

I don't know how but always it's more of you
and less of me.

Hey the point is you miss me, no?

Now don't try to hide,

I already know.

-"Okay fine I miss you really I do."

Why don't you say so??

Don't worry I am not going anywhere,

'I love you' is the thing everywhere I'll scream,

God! Yes, it's always more of you less of me.

In my heart in my soul everywhere you play a
beautiful role,

In my reality in my dreams

It's always more of you and less of me.

Not too old

I heard a wierd sound at the door,

Knock knock, who's there?

Oh it's my heart,

That's not mine anymore.

: Please let me be in

It's me your heart here.

Walking on love path is so tough,

I don't want to be broken into layers.

: I can't do anything now,

It's already too late.

Now 'Guilty pleasure' is the only thing,

That we have in our fate.

: Look listen here,you can't handle the broken me,

Pink sky, birds fly when your lover passes by,

This is only a fantasy dream.

: I am mature enough to know what's right and
wrong,

I am happy, that person makes me strong.

I really don't fear

because Loving is a path mixed with laughters
and tears.

: Why can't you admit that you too are scared of
heartbreak,

Loosing that person is something that I (your heart)
can't take.

Why do you want to continue walking on this path?

Even when you know the consequences, you know
the aftermath.

: Whenever he says 'I love you' it get dissolved in the
deepening twilight just like a solvent,

Then I start grinning like an idiot and to prevent
blushing... I say something irrelevant.

Yes! Yes! I know the aftermath is bitter,

But loving; it's just filled with enchanted glitters.

I know all the glitters are not gold,

But please let me win once,

I want to prove that the idea of old school love in this
modern era,

Is not too old,

Is not too old.

See, You are smiling - a song fiction

And yes it's magical, yes.

When you see those tangled relationship threads getting lines which were once a total mess.

And yes this is a happy sign when you start loving a person whom once you have hated for no reason,

and now that person is so important for you,

now that person is the rain in your love's season.

//Zindagi ne ki hai kaisi saazishen

Poori hui dil ki wo farmaaishein

Maangi dua ek tujh tak hai pohnchi, Parvardigaara

Deewaangi ki hdd mene nochi, Parvardigaara. //

Isn't it funny now??

You can't even spend a single minute without thinking about that person.

Have you wondered how??

This feeling is totally on another level,

Now you don't want to let this love leave, Never Ever.

Everything in you is changed now,

you blushes everytime you hear there name,

haha com'on tell na!!

That the fire of your love is catching the flame.

//Ye fitoor mera; laya mujhko hai tere kareeb

Ye fitoor mera; rehmat teri

Ye fitoor mera; maine bdla hai mera naseeb

Ye fitoor mera; chaahat teri//

Well, now you miss them everyday more than yesterday.

Your heart want to scream out loud but you don't have words to explain,

you hesitate to say.

But still that person gets it even before you explained,

OMG! If you have someone like this,

you don't know what you have gained.

//Dheeme dheeme jal rhi thi khwaahishein

Dil mein dbi ghutt rhi farmaaishein

Bn k dhuaan wo tujh tak ja pohnchi, Parvardigaara

Kese suni tuhne meri khaamoshi? Parvardigaara//

You are the one who teases them the whole day,

but still at the end you don't want them to say goodbye,

you want them to Stay.

If this isn't love then what is this?

You can't even go to sleep without there good
night wish.

Is is love that have changed the stubborn you,

all these feelings, all this love, everything seems
like new.

//Ye fitoor mera; laya mujhko hai tere kareeb.

Ye fitoor mera; mene badla re mera naseeb

Ye fitoor mera; rehmat teri. //

See, You are smiling

coz you have already gone through this love
through this pain.

And the main thing is as you read more and more
the only thing coming in your mind is there name

//Ye fitoor mera; chaahat teri//

Parvardigaara

Song - YE FITOOR MERA (Movie- FITOOR)

They have never left-
A song fiction

Oops! We can't stop the time,

and if somehow I left soon then for you it should be fine.

Everyone in this world comes to leave,

and the void it creates can never be filled those who knows; knows..

for others it's hard to believe.

But still they are with us loving us and making us strong,

correct me if I am wrong.

//Main rahoon ya na rahoon,

Tum mujh mein kahin baaki rehna,

Mujhe neend aaye jo aakhri,

Tum khwaabon mein aate rehna,

Bs itna hai tumse kehna, bs itna hai tumse kehna//

Humans are not immortal,

but yes the love is.

Somehow using the magic of nature those loved ones comes to us,

and this sign is something that we should not miss.

They'll be keeping an eye on you from the heaven,
They'll be loving you the whole time,
whether it is week's day 1 Or 7.

//Kisi roz baarish jo aaye,
Smjh lena boondon mein mai hoon,
Subah dhoop tujhko staaye,
Smjh lena kirno mein main hoon//

We are use to listen to them,
talk to them everyday,
but it feel so wrong when we realise that
the person is not with you anymore to say you 'Hey'.
But somewhere all the time you can hear their voice
in your ear,
and you'll feel that they are not away from you
but so near.

//Kuch kahoon ya na kahoon,
Tum mujhko sda sunn te rehna,
Bs itna hai tumse kehna//

Then those sleeplessness nights,
that regret that when you met them for the last time
why didn't you hugged them tight.
That illusion that they are on the door,
That stubbornness of your heart to not accept that
they are no more.

But in your dreams when you'll complain them

that since they had gone you hadn't slept,

they'll embrace you with their presence and

will make you feel like

"THEY HAVE NEVER LEFT"

//Main dikhu ya na dikhun,

Tum mujhko mehsoos krna,

Bs itna hai tumse kehna,

Bs itna hai tumse kehna.

Main rahoon ya na rahoon,

Tum mujh mein kahin baaki rehna//

Song- Main Rahoon Ya Na Rahoon

143 Pages Apart- A song fiction

Life is so unpredictable.

You don't know what next will happen now.

But i got a constant support system in form you you.

Haha! I know it's just woww.

I want to spend my whole time with you,

I want to tell how much do i love you,

and again in this there's nothing new.

//Pal pal mera tere he sng bitaana hai,

Apni wafaaon se tujhe sjana hai,

Dil chahta hai tujhe kitna, batana hai,

Tere saath he mera thikaana hai//

I have travelled alot in your love place,

I am so tired but still you can see this charm,

this smile on my face.

I wish you was here with me,

but the only place I can meet you is in my dream.

//Ab thak chuke hai ye kadam,

Chl ghar chlein mere humdum.

Da umra pyaar na hoga km,

Chl ghar chlein mere humdum//

I crave for your presence,

I crave for your sight,

I collect the starts and draw you

between them every single night.

I love it so much that i simply burns the sunrise in my

dreams

just to make the night longer,

we are far away from each other but with every

passing day

this feel becomes stronger & stronger.

//Sang tere pyaar ka jahaan basaana hai,

Jismein rhe tum aur hum,

Chal ghar chlein mere humdum.

Mere raho tum, Aur tere hum,

Chal ghar chlein mere humdum.//

Maybe we just found forever at wrong time,

and someday this world will put us together again.

And I guess that will be fine.

Will you believe if I say that

I hadn't slept as I was waiting for you since so long??

Will you please embrace me with your hug and sing

for me my favorite song.??

//Khidki pe tu khda dekhe hai rssta mera,

Aakhon ko he pal mile yahi ik mnzar tera.

Bss ab teri baahon mein jaaanam sojana hai,

Jaage huye raaton ke hum,

Chl ghar chlein mere humdum.//

Whenever I open the book of my heart,

it shows your place 143 pages apart.

Do you know what does this mean?

Exactly it's nothing new as

•1 4 3 = I LOVE YOU•

Finally you came to meet me,

but i fell from the bed and missed the scene..

Yeah you got it right,

he is still 143 pages apart,

it was just in my dream.

//Mere raho tum aur tere hum,

Chal ghar chlein mere humdum.

Daumra pyaar na hoga kum,

Chal ghar chlein,Mere humdum.//

Song- Chal ghar chalein (MALANG)